CAVEKID
Birthday

Cathy Breisacher
Illustrated by **Roland Garrigue**

ini Charlesbridge

To Kelly DiPucchio and David Greenberg—C. B.

To my godson Barth—R. G.

Published by Charlesbridge
85 Main Street
Watertown, MA 02472
(617) 926-0329
www.charlesbridge.com

Library of Congress Cataloging-in-Publication Data
Names: Breisacher, Cathy, author. | Garrigue, Roland, 1979– illustrator.
Title: Cavekid birthday / Cathy Breisacher ; illustrated by Roland Garrigue.
Description: Watertown, MA : Charlesbridge, [2018] | Summary: Caveboy and Cavegirl were born on
    the same day, in neighboring caves, and every year they celebrated and played together—but
    this year they are each looking for the perfect gift for their friend at Caveman's Collectibles.
Identifiers: LCCN 2017033093 (print) | LCCN 2017045905 (ebook) | ISBN 9781632896964 (ebook) | ISBN
    9781632896957 (ebook pdf) | ISBN 9781580898768 (reinforced for library use)
Subjects: LCSH: Cave dwellers—Juvenile fiction. | Birthdays—Juvenile fiction. | Gifts—Juvenile fiction.
    | Friendship—Juvenile fiction. | CYAC: Cave dwellers—Fiction. | Birthdays—Fiction. | Gifts—Fiction.
    | Friendship—Fiction. | LCGFT: Picture books.
Classification: LCC PZ7.B7487 (ebook) | LCC PZ7.B7487 Cav 2018 (print) | DDC
[E]—dc23
LC record available at https://lccn.loc.gov/2017033093

Printed in China
(hc) 10 9 8 7 6 5 4 3 2 1

Display type set in LosLana Niu Pro by Bruno Jara & Luciano Vergara and
    BaileywickJF-Festive by Jason Walcott/Jukebox
Text type set in LosLana Niu Pro by Bruno Jara & Luciano Vergara
Color separations by Colourscan Print Co Pte Ltd, Singapore
Printed by 1010 Printing International Limited in Huizhou, Guangdong, China
Production supervision by Brian G. Walker
Designed by Martha MacLeod Sikkema

Caveboy and Cavegirl were born on the same day, in side-by-side caves.

In no time at all, they became the best of friends.

Every year they celebrated their birthday together.

And every day they played hide-and-seek . . .

searched for shapes in clouds . . .

and raced their pets.

Eventually Caveboy discovered that he loved . . . rocks!

Shiny rocks. Rough rocks. Stacking rocks and building rocks.

He showed his rocks to Cavegirl and taught her to play stone toss.

Cavegirl discovered that she loved something, too . . . tools!
Pointy tools. Wide tools. Planting tools and painting tools.
She showed her tools to Caveboy and taught him to create
masterpieces on cave walls.

Soon it would be their birthday again.

"Need gift for Caveboy," thought Cavegirl.

She made a rock statue, but Bear ruined it.

She painted a picture, but it was stuck to the wall.

So she went to Caveman's Collectibles and peered inside.

There she spotted the perfect gift.

"Box for Caveboy's rocks!"

"Make trade?" asked Caveman.

"Trade?" said Cavegirl. "Have nothing to trade, except . . . *tools*!"

"Ten tools for box," grunted Caveman.

"Ten?" asked Cavegirl. "Me only have ten!"

She paused for a moment.

"Bye-bye, tools," she said. "Caveboy will love gift."

Meanwhile Caveboy was busy thinking about their birthday, too.

"Need gift for Cavegirl," thought Caveboy.

He made a rake, but Mammoth ruined it.

He painted a picture, but it was too heavy to move.

So he went to Caveman's Collectibles and peered inside.

There he spotted the perfect gift.

"Box for Cavegirl's tools!"

"Make trade?" asked Caveman.

"Trade?" said Caveboy. "Have nothing to trade, except . . . *rocks*!"

"Twenty rocks for box," grunted Caveman.

"Twenty?" asked Caveboy. "Me only have twenty!"

He paused for a moment.

"Bye-bye, rocks," he said. "Cavegirl will love gift."

The day before their birthday, Cavegirl and Caveboy
jumped up and down.
"Can't wait," said Cavegirl.
"Open presents now!" said Caveboy.
They tore off the wrappings.

Cavegirl bit her lip.

Caveboy scratched his head.

"Me traded tools to get rock box for you," Cavegirl said softly.

"And me traded rocks to get toolbox for you," Caveboy said.

"What now?" asked Caveboy.

They thought for a minute and began to play.

The boxes were just right for . . .

playing hide-and-seek . . .

searching for shapes in clouds . . .

and racing their pets.

But eventually Caveboy missed his rocks.
Cavegirl missed her tools, too.

So the next day they headed for Caveman's Collectibles.

"Need rocks for Caveboy," said Cavegirl.

"Need tools for Cavegirl," said Caveboy.

"Make trade?" they asked.

"Trade?" said Caveman.

"For rocks, we clean store," said Caveboy.

"For tools, we paint store," said Cavegirl.

"Ta-da!"

"Me like," said Caveman. "Trade good."

"Birthday good," said Caveboy.

"Birthday *very* good," said Cavegirl.